A SUPER WEIRD! MYSTERY

"My pencil case is a time machine"

Jim Smith

Welcome to Donut

Hello and welcome to another Super Weird mystery! My name is Yoshi Fujikawa and I live on Donut Island.

Donut Island is a completely round island with a giant hole in the middle of it. Which is probably why it's called Donut Island.

Donut Island

me

These are my best friends:

Rhubarb Plonsky   Melvin Pebble

Together we work at our school newspaper,
The Daily Donut, investigating all the
Super Weird mysteries that happen here
on Donut Island.

Here are a couple of the mysteries, just to give you a flavour:

Once, this giant slime monster tried to eat all the kids from school.

But we zapped it with a moon beam and it exploded into a billion tiny droplets.

7

Another time, Rhubarb's dad, who was eaten by a crocodile, came back as a ghost. Then he got shrunk to the size of a can of Donut Soda.

Anyway, that's the end of this book.
I know there's loads more pages, but
they're all completely blank.
Hope you enjoyed
the story!

THE
END

Only joking, you can turn the page now.

Donut Tube

It all started one Saturday when I was sitting at home watching telly.

I say watching telly, I wasn't really. I was staring at my phone.

Have I mentioned my new phone? I love it.

cool donut logo on back

Donut Phone Corp™

'Probably better write up that mystery Rhubarb's waiting for,' I said, not that there was anyone else in the room to hear me. I put down my phone and picked up my notepad.

My phone did a little beep and stared up at me all sadly.

'Oh go on then,' I said, putting my notepad back down and picking up the phone again.

I looked at the Donut Tube logo on the screen - there was a tiny number one in the corner of it.

Donut Tube, in case you don't already know, is this app that lets you upload your videos for other people to watch.

I clicked on the logo. 'Congratulations! You have five new followers!' said a little message that popped up at the top of the screen.

'That means I've got thirty-seven followers now,' I said to myself. 'Time for a new video to celebrate!'

I pressed record on my phone and smiled into the camera. 'Hi, this Yoshi Fujikawa from The Daily Donut. Just sitting here watching the telly - as you do!'

I tried to think of something else to say, but couldn't come up with anything.

I pressed the green button and my video uploaded to Donut Tube. Straightaway a little heart floated up from the bottom of the screen and a comment appeared.

'Great video, Yoshi!' it said. The person who'd written it was called Sonu789.

'Good old Sonu, she always leaves a comment!' I said. Sonu is a girl from my class at school, by the way.

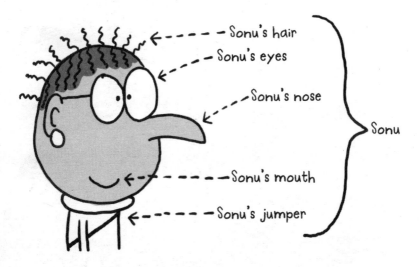

I liked Sonu's comment and typed 'Thanx Sonu!' underneath it.

Sonu immediately liked my comment and wrote 'Thanx for the like Yoshi!'

I thought about typing 'Thanx for your thanx!' under that, but decided not to. You've got to play it cool on Donut Tube.

Instead I scrolled through some of my other videos. There was one of me, Rhubarb and Melvin from a couple of days ago when we were investigating . . .

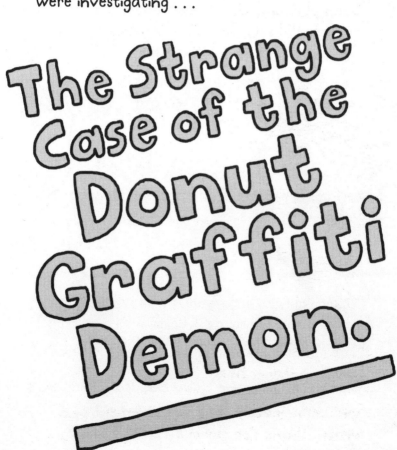

The Strange Case of the Donut Graffiti Demon.

About that

The Donut Graffiti Demon is this person who's been going round Donut spraying strange words on to the sides of buildings.

I pressed play on the video.

'We've found a new one!' I was whispering. I pointed my phone at a brick wall. Sprayed on to it were the words, 'MILK CARTON'.

'That's the third one this week,' said Rhubarb's voice. 'What could they all mean?'

The phone moved across to face Melvin and he raised his eyebrows. 'Stay tuned to find out!' he said, and the video ended.

'Classic vid,' I said to myself.

Just then, my dad stuck his head into the living room. He had a bit of old spider web hanging off his hair and his jumper was all dusty.

'You're not on that blooming phone again are you?' he said. 'You'll turn into one if you carry on like that.'

I clicked my phone off and stuffed it into my pocket. Immediately it buzzed. It was probably another comment on my new video.

I pulled it back out of my pocket and was just about to check the screen when my dad stuck his hand into the living room too. It was holding an old shoe box.

My dad gave the shoe box a waggle, and even though I really wanted to read my new comment, the shoe box won.

'What's in that shoe box?' I asked, stuffing my phone back into my pocket.

'My smelly eraser collection from when I was a kid,' he said. 'I found it up in the attic, thought you might like them.'

He lifted the lid off the shoe box and I spotted something fizzle inside.

'Static electricity,' mumbled my dad,
who must've spotted the fizzle too.
'Probably from the pylon.'

I don't know if
you know this,
but our house
sits slap bang
underneath
an enormous
electricity
pylon.

I jumped off the sofa and strolled over
to my dad. Then I peered into the shoe box
and gasped. But only so you'd read the next
chapter.

Smelly erasers

Inside the shoebox were loads of smelly erasers. Which wasn't very surprising really, seeing as my dad had already told me that.

Smelly erasers, in case you don't know, are erasers that smell like the things they look like.

There were all different types - a banana, a bunch of grapes, a cherry lipstick, an ice lolly . . . I mean, I could go on, but I don't want to bore you.

I reached out to grab one when my phone started to ring. I pulled it out of my pocket and saw Rhubarb's name so pressed the answer button.

'Hi Rubes,' I said.

'The Donut Graffiti Demon has struck again!' said Rhubarb, just like that, without even saying hello. That's what Rhubarb's like - she's completely obsessed with mysteries.

'Forget about the Donut Graffiti Demon,' I said, and I explained about The Case of the Fizzling Smelly Erasers.

'Interesting,' said Rhubarb. 'Bring them down to Brenda the Hut so me and Melvin can have a look.'

'Will do,' I said, grabbing the shoe box off my dad, pouring the smelly erasers into my pencil case and heading for the front door.

Donut Cola Factory

I strolled down Donut High Street and stopped when I got to Donut Diner at the end. Just across from it stood the ugly looking factory they'd been building there for the last few months.

'Opening next week - Donut Cola Factory!' said a poster taped inside one of its windows.

I whipped my phone out and pointed it at the factory, then pressed record. 'Looks like there's a new cola factory coming next week,' I said. 'Sounds good to me!'

I posted the video to Donut Tube, making sure to tag @TheDonutColaFactoryCompany, and carried on my way, past the giant hole in the middle of the island.

Nobody knew how the hole had got there, or how deep it was either. I peered into the enormous crater and imagined falling to the bottom of it.

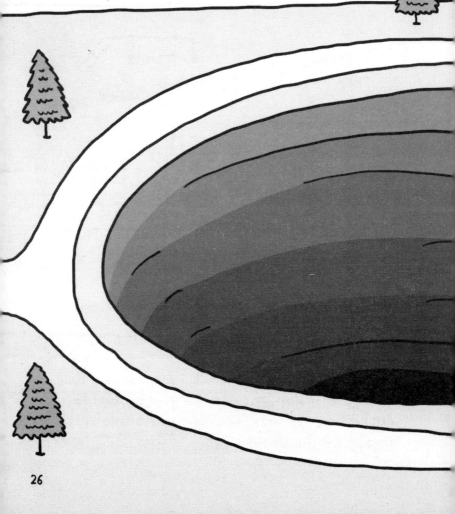

'Thank goodness that's never going to happen,' I mumbled to myself as I walked up to Brenda the Hut, which is the name of The Daily Donut's headquarters.

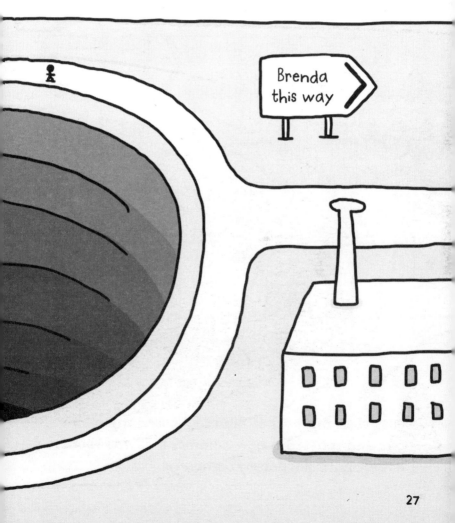

Brenda the Hut is this little hut in the tiny forest behind Donut Juniors. It's named after Brenda the dinner lady from Donut Juniors.

'There you are!' said Melvin as I walked through the door. 'Where are these smelly erasers then?'

Brenda the Hut

In memory of Brenda the dinner lady, who loved a leftover.

Just then my pocket buzzed. I pulled my phone out and spotted a new comment. It was from @TheDonutColaFactoryCompany!

'So glad you're excited about our new factory!'
it said. 'Come and visit us when we're open!'

'Thanx, @TheDonutColaFactoryCompany!'
I wrote underneath. 'Will do!'

I scrolled through a few of my older videos,
checking if they had any new likes I hadn't
spotted.

'Hello-o?' said Rhubarb, knocking on my head
like it was a front door. 'Honestly, you and
that blimming phone. I miss the old Yoshi
with his little black notepad.'

29

'I'm doing this for The Daily Donut, you know,' I said, pointing at my phone. 'We've got thirty-seven followers now. If that keeps going we're gonna be famous!'

'Who wants to be famous?' said Rhubarb. 'We're detectives, not Donut Tube stars.'

I shook my head. 'Rhubarb, Rhubarb, Rhubarb,' I said. 'Don't you understand? There's nothing better than being a Donut Tube star.'

I carried on scrolling through the Donut Tube app and clicked on a video. 'Check this bloke out, for example.'

Roland's Room

A big round face popped up on the screen. 'Welcome to Roland's Room!' said the teenager who owned it. 'Today I've been sent this brand new scooter from the amazing people at Donut Scooters!'

Rhubarb rolled her eyes. 'Ugh, he's one of those Unboxers, isn't he,' she said.

'An Unboxer? What's that when it's at home?' asked Melvin in his old granny voice, and Rhubarb chuckled.

'It's when you get sent free stuff to open in your Donut Tube videos,' I explained. 'But you can only be one if you've got loads of followers.'

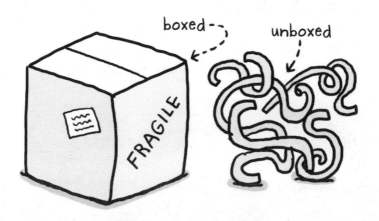

boxed --→

unboxed

FRAGILE

Melvin nodded. 'Oh yeah, I've seen those videos,' he said.

'Roland's Room is the best,' I said. 'I wish I could be like him.'

Rhubarb did a yawn. 'Could you just show us your smelly erasers already?' she said.

'Fine,' I said, clicking off my phone and pulling my pencil case out of my rucksack. 'Behold: the world famous fizzling smelly erasers!'

I did a little sniggle to myself about how I was talking about them. After all, they were only a pile of old smelly erasers with a bit of pylon fizzle zapping around inside them, weren't they.

doesn't realise
what's going
to happen

'Come on, let's have a sniff,' said Rhubarb, who's a big smeller. That makes it sound like she stinks. What I mean is, she likes smelling stuff.

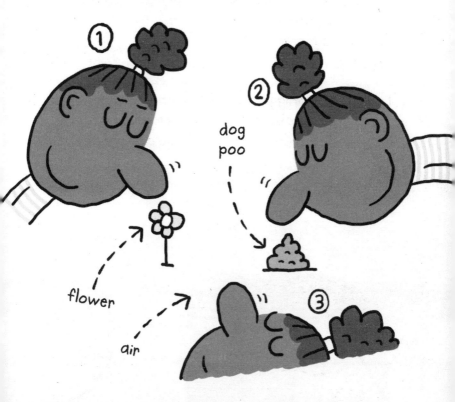

'Now hang on there just a millisecond, young lady,' I said in MY old granny voice. 'I haven't had a chance to give them a sniffle myself yet!'

The only problem was, Rhubarb wasn't chuckling.

'Why aren't you laughing at my old granny voice?' I said.

'Face it, Yoshi,' said Melvin. 'It just isn't that funny.'

Just then, I spotted something on the shelf behind Melvin where we keep the little collectables from some of our old Super Weird mysteries. For example, there's a jam jar full of green slime from that time the slime monster tried to eat us all.

And a little clay dog Mrs Terrible from the pottery shop made that looks kind of like a crocodile. That was from The Mystery of Rhubarb's Dad Coming Back From The Dead.

Next to the pottery crocodile dog sat a completely plain, rectangle-shaped white eraser.

'What's that boring old normal eraser doing up there?' I said. I couldn't remember it being part of any of our mysteries.

'Oh that,' said Rhubarb. 'Nobody knows. It's always been up there, it came with the hut.'

'I call it Brenda the Eraser,' said Melvin, and Rhubarb chuckled - again!

I grabbed Brenda the Eraser and plopped her into my pencil case. 'She'll be happier in here with all the other erasers,' I said. I'm like that - I feel sorry for things like erasers.

Rhubarb tapped me on the shoulder. 'How about a sniff of one of those smelly ones, then?' she said, and I pulled out a dinosaur-shaped smelly eraser.

And I know this sounds like I'm trying to get you to read the next chapter, but that really was one of the stupidest things I've ever done.

Ridge nails

I held the eraser up and Rhubarb stared at it. Or at least that's what I thought she was doing.

'You've got very unusual fingernails, haven't you,' she said. She wasn't staring at the eraser at all. She was staring at my fingernails!

'No,' I said. 'They're completely normal.'

Melvin grabbed my hand and zoomed his eyeballs in on my fingernails. 'They are a bit weird,' he said. 'Very ridgy.'

'They are NOT!' I said, peering down at them myself. I had to admit, they were a tiny bit on the ridgy side. 'Anyway, forget about my fingernails. Let's smell this smelly eraser!'

I held it up again and we all leaned our noses in. There was the sound of all three of us taking a sniff and then . . .

KASPLONKLE!

Now, I don't know if you've ever smelt a
dinosaur smelly eraser before, but it smells
exactly like wet dog.

'Poowee, whose dog got wet?' said Rhubarb,
sniffing the air.

I looked around. Instead of being inside
Brenda the Hut, we were standing in what
seemed to be a giant nest. Dotted around
us were about seven enormous eggs
the size of rugby balls.

'What in the name of . . .' I said, too shocked
to come up with a name.

'What are all these rugby balls doing in this nest?' said Melvin, looking down at his feet.

'They're eggs, you dimwit,' said Rhubarb, as a bead of sweat ran down her forehead. This wasn't the tiny forest behind Donut Juniors. It was more like a boiling hot rainforest.

I whipped my phone out and pressed record. 'Yoshi Fujikawa from The Daily Donut here,' I said, staring into the camera. 'It seems we've been zapped into some kind of giant nest. Stay tuned for more!'

I pressed the upload button and a big
red cross appeared on the screen.
'No connection,' it said underneath.

'Oh bums,' I said, giving my phone a shake
and trying it again. But it still didn't work.

'Lemme see that eraser,' said Rhubarb,
snatching the little dinosaur out of my
hand. She gave it another sniff with her
expert hooter and it fizzled. 'Interesting . . .'

'You can say that
again,' said Melvin,
picking up one
of the rugby
ball eggs.

Rhubarb stroked her chin. 'I think we might've been zapped back to the time of the dinosaurs,' she said, all relaxed and everything like it was no big deal.

'Excuse me?' I said, looking up from my screen. I stared at the dinosaur eraser in her hand. 'Have you gone doolally or something?'

Rhubarb shook her head. 'It's all to do with noses,' she said.

The nose lectures

'Please, not one of your boring old nose lectures,' said Melvin.

I kind of knew how he felt, to be honest. Rhubarb is ALWAYS going on about noses and smelling stuff. She's obsessed!

Rhubarb opened her mouth. 'When I was a little kid, I used to visit my grandfather in his workshop. He was a clock maker, you know.'

'What sort of clocks did he make?' I asked, mostly just to be polite.

'Grandfather clocks, of course,' said Rhubarb. 'Anyway, he had piles of sawdust and chopped-in-half planks of wood stacked up everywhere.'

47

Melvin gave the giant egg he was holding a little tap. 'Is this really the time for a story about your grandad's shed?'

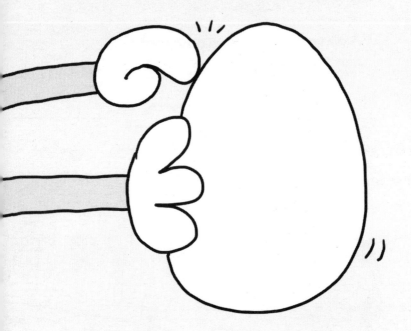

'I loved the smell of that wood,' said Rhubarb, completely ignoring Melvin. 'Whenever I smell the smell of it now, I'm immediately transported straight back to his workshop.'

'Argh, I knew this was a nose lecture!' cried Melvin. He was holding his egg next to his ear now and giving it a little shake.

'What, you're actually transported back to your grandad's workshop?' I asked Rhubarb.

'Of course not,' she said, doing a little chuckle. 'I meant it just reminds me of it.' She focused her eyes on the smelly eraser she was holding. 'I think the same thing must've happened with this dinosaur. Except this time, we really were transported.'

Well, I almost dropped my phone into a giant pile of poo right there on the spot.

'By the power of Great Aunt Kanako,' I said. 'Are you telling me we've been zapped back to the time of dinosaurs?!'

Kanako is my dad's auntie, by the way.

Aunt Kanako

Rhubarb nodded. 'The fizzle from that electricity pylon seems to have fused with this ordinary smelly eraser and turned it into a ... well, a time machine,' she said.

I was still holding my pencil case and I peered into it, wondering if any of my dad's other smelly erasers could zap us through time as well.

Just then, Melvin's egg started to wobble in his hand.

I zoomed my eyes in on it as a crack appeared. A piece of the eggshell fell off and a beaky little nose poked through the hole.

'B-b-baby dino!' cried Melvin, dropping the egg. It cracked in half and a miniature T-Rex crawled out, blinked, then did a yawn.

'Ahh, he's a little cutie!' said Rhubarb.

The baby dino was covered in tiny wet feathers. 'He's a little stinky too,' I said. 'I think that must be the wet-dog smell.'

Suddenly I heard a noise behind us. 'What was that noise?' said Melvin.

'Yeah, what was that noise?' I said.

'Sounded like some kind of giant footstep,' said Rhubarb.

I twizzled round on the spot and started screaming.

Mummy T-Rex

The reason I was screaming was that a giant, full-sized T-Rex was stomping towards us with its mouth wide open.

'I think it's the baby's mum!' screeched Melvin.

'And she looks kind of hungry!' cried Rhubarb.

'Quick, this way!' I shouted, heading in the direction of Donut High Street.

You know when you're running through a rainforest with a T-Rex chasing after you and you realise Donut High Street probably won't get invented for another sixty-five million years?

THAT.

I swivelled my head around, trying to look for something familiar. 'Hey, I think I recognise that stone over there,' I said, pointing at a small brown pebble. 'I remember seeing it on the pavement outside the pizza shop once.'

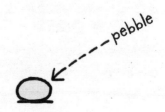

pebble

'What good is that going to do us?'
screamed Rhubarb.

A giant claw reached out to grab her, and
I guessed it was the T-Rex's. That or Melvin
hadn't cut his nails for a while.

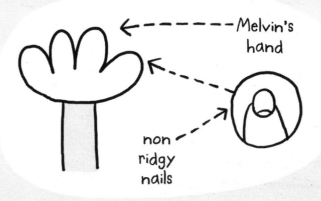

Melvin's
hand

non
ridgy
nails

A cloud hovered in the sky above a monkey
puzzle tree and I pointed at it. 'That cloud,'
I said. 'I swear I've seen it floating above
Donut Library. That means we're on the
High Street!'

'So what if we are?' cried Melvin. 'It doesn't
make any difference to Mrs T-Rex. She's
gonna gobble us up either way!'

Not if we're clever about it,' I said, speeding past Rhubarb and towards the end of the High Street, where the giant hole in the middle of Donut Island is.

Rhubarb caught up with me again. 'What are you thinking, Yosh?' she asked.

'If we run straight towards the giant hole then skid to a stop just before the edge, hopefully the T-Rex will carry on going.'

'What, and fall into the hole?' cried Melvin, who was just behind us. 'But then that poor little baby dino won't have a mum.'

The T-Rex snapped its mouth shut, missing Melvin's bum by a millimetre.

'Second thoughts, I'm sure it'll be fine,' he said.

We were getting to the part of the rainforest that'd usually be the end of Donut High Street.

'That's funny,' I said. 'No hole.'

'I've just thought of something,' said Rhubarb, looking worried. I mean, she'd been looking worried anyway, but now she looked REALLY worried.

'What have you thought of?' I said.
I wasn't sure I wanted to hear it.

'Maybe the hole doesn't exist yet,' said
Rhubarb. 'We ARE millions of years back
in time, after all.'

My legs were beginning to get a tiny bit
worn out. 'Oh flip-flops, I hadn't thought
of that.'

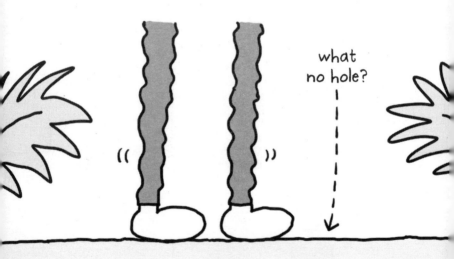

what
no hole?

'Now what?!' cried Melvin. The T-Rex
was still snapping at his bum.

The hand I was using to carry my pencil case was getting pretty sweaty by now, and I was worried I might drop all my erasers, so I swapped the pencil case to the other, less sweaty hand.

sweaty

less sweaty

'Hang on a minute,' I said. 'I think I might've had another idea!'

'Then tell us it already!' cried Rhubarb.

The Smelly eraser idea

'Well, seeing as that dinosaur eraser zapped us back to dinosaur times, maybe one of the other ones could zap us back to normal times,' I said, all in one go, just like that.

Melvin nodded. 'I like it,' he shouted. 'Grab a eraser. Let's do this. Like, NOW!'

I unzipped my pencil case and stuck my sweaty hand in. I felt like one of those claw games at the arcade that drop the thing they're picking up every time you have a go.

'Got one!' I cried, pulling my hand out. Inside it was a cola-can smelly eraser.

Unfortunately, due to my sweaty hand being ever-so-slightly sticky, a couple of other erasers had stuck to my skin too. But not enough to stay there for very long.

The smelly erasers dropped off my hand and landed on the rainforest floor. 'Brenda the Eraser!' cried Melvin, and I spotted a plain, rectangle-shaped eraser land on a leaf and do a little fizzle.

'Forget about her,' shouted Rhubarb. 'She's just a plain old non-smelly eraser.'

'How dare you talk about Brenda like that!'
cried Melvin. The T-Rex opened its mouth
and roared. 'OK, forget about her,' he said.
'She'll be all right.'

Just then, the sky turned dark and a
strange crackle echoed through the air.
I looked up and spotted a giant firework,
heading straight for Donut Island.

'What in the name of . . .' I said, still not
able to come up with a name.

I held up the little cola can and leaned my nose towards it. Rhubarb did the same. Melvin was just behind us. 'Hurry up!' I shouted, and he sped up, his schnozzle hurtling towards the eraser.

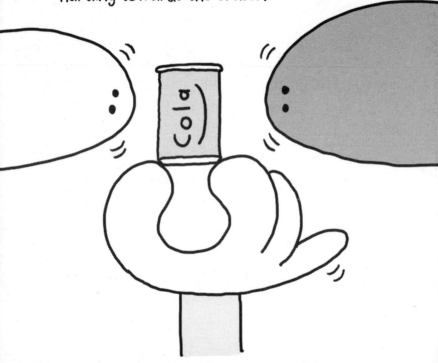

The T-Rex skidded to a stop and stared into the sky. 'Uh-oh that doesn't look good,' it said, and for a millisecond I wondered if dinosaurs could speak English. Then I stopped wondering about that and did a sniff.

KASPLONKLE AGAIN!

Suddenly I was back on good old normal Donut Island. I looked around and spotted the Donut Cola Factory, standing on the edge of the giant hole.

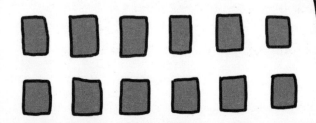

'Your plan - it worked!' cried Rhubarb. 'We've kasplonkled ourselves back to the present!'

'Somebody should make a film called that,' I said.

Then I remembered something. 'Hey, do you remember how there wasn't a giant hole back in dinosaur times?' I said.

Rhubarb nodded. 'Yeah, so what?'

I looked down and realised I was . . .

"FLOATING" ABOVE THE "GIANT HOLE!"

I say floating, it was more like I was falling, actually.

'Where's Melvin?' screamed Rhubarb, who was hovering next to me.

I say hovering, she was falling too.

I looked around again. 'He's not here!' I cried. 'Maybe he didn't sniff the cola can!'

It was weird, we were falling really slowly like we were in a cartoon or something. Which was good, because it gave us time to have this chat.

'I can't believe I'm falling into the hole!' I screamed. 'I was only just imagining that this morning.'

I know we were falling slowly, but I was really beginning to push my luck now.

'Quick, smell this!' shouted Rhubarb, holding up the dinosaur eraser, and we both took a whiff.

KASPLONKLE #3

'Where the blooming . . . blimming . . . GAAAH!!!' cried Melvin, as my and Rhubarb's bums landed on the rainforest floor with a bump.

Melvin was still running for his life.

I scrabbled back to my feet and zoomed after him with Rhubarb, away from the middle of the giant hole. Or where it would be in a million years or so, anyway.

The giant firework was still heading straight towards us (and the T-Rex as well, who was looking more worried than hungry all of a sudden).

I skidded to a stop behind a tree, hoping we were far enough away from where the hole was going to be in the future.

'Let's try this again,' I said, holding up the cola-can eraser, and we all leaned our noses in and took a sniff.

KASPLONKLE

#4

We were back on good old Donut Island again, this time on solid ground.

I stuffed my pencil case into my rucksack and leaned against the wall of the Donut Cola Factory, kissing its bricks. 'I'll never smell another smelly eraser again,' I said.

Rhubarb chuckled, then she sniffed the air. 'That's funny,' she said. 'The air smells of cola.'

I stared up at the giant chimneys poking out of the factory roof. Thick brown steam was pouring out of them.

'Super Weird,' said Melvin. 'I thought the Donut Cola Factory wasn't opening until next week.'

Just then a man strolled past reading a newspaper. I zoomed my eyes in on the date in the corner of the page and gasped.

'About that,' I said, turning to my friends. 'It IS next week.'

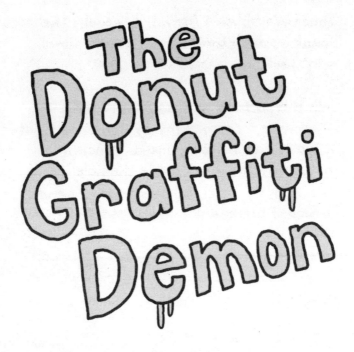

The Donut Graffiti Demon

Rhubarb looked at the cola-can smelly
eraser I was still holding in my hand.
'The cola can,' she said, then she peered up
at the factory. 'The smell must've zapped
us forward in time to when the Donut
Cola Factory was open.'

'Curse those smelly erasers!' said Melvin.

'I'm just glad that T-Rex is gone,'
said Rhubarb.

'And that massive firework,' I said. 'It was heading straight for . . .' I stared at the giant hole and gasped.

'What is it, Yosh?' asked Melvin.

'It wasn't a firework,' I said. 'It was a meteor. That's what made the hole!'

I whipped my phone out and started filming. 'Yoshi Fujikawa here,' I said. 'Breaking news from The Daily Donut gang. We've finally cracked The Case of Why There's A Giant Hole In The Middle Of Donut Island!'

Rhubarb shrieked, completely ruining my video. She was pointing at the Donut Cola Factory. I zoomed my eyes in and saw an old man standing there. He was holding a can of yellow spray paint and writing the word 'WATER BOTTLE' on the brick wall.

'It's the Donut Graffiti Demon,' cried Melvin.

I peered into my phone's camera. 'Gotta go, Super Weird fans!' I said, pressing the upload button.

A big red cross appeared on the screen.

'That's strange,' I said. 'No connection again.' I could understand why it wouldn't connect in the dinosaur times, but why wasn't it working now?

'Forget your blooming connection,' said Rhubarb. 'Look at what the Donut Graffiti Demon's doing!'

I looked up and spotted the old man floating a couple of centimetres off the ground. 'How's he doing that?' I said.

'Who cares,' cried Melvin. 'He's getting away!'

Sure enough, the old man had seen us and was hovering off down Donut High Street.

'Who is this guy?' cried Rhubarb as we zigzagged after him.

The old man hover-skidded to a stop at the bottom of the steps that led up to the entrance to Donut Museum.

'Look at him go!' I said, as he hovered up the steps three at a time and through the revolving doors.

'We've got him now!' said Melvin, as we zoomed after him, into the Prehistoric Hall.

And that's when another chapter started . . .

Archie Clamp

It was dark and gloomy inside the Prehistoric Hall. Glass cases stood all round the edge, a single spotlight shining inside each one.

The walls were covered in scaffolding, and in one of the walls a doorway-shaped hole had been smashed through, leading to the room next door.

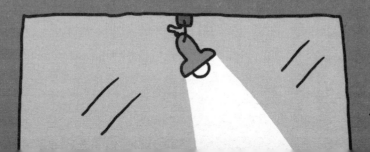

'Sorry for any inconvenience while we make some improvements to the Prehistoric Hall,' said a sign sticky-taped to one of the scaffolding poles.

The Donut Graffiti Demon was standing in front of the nearest glass case, peering into it with his back facing us.

There was a collection of amber stones inside the case. You know, the sort you see in films when there's a mosquito frozen inside with a smidgen of dinosaur DNA in its dried-up blood.

The old man swivelled round and smiled,
revealing two rows of glowing white teeth.
And when I say glowing I mean
GLOWING. It was like each tooth
had a little rectangle-shaped
lightbulb inside it.

'Looks like The Daily
Donut gang caught me,'
he said.

Rhubarb gasped. 'How do you know who we are?' she asked.

'I know everything about you,' said the man.

Melvin peered up at him. 'Oh yeah?' he said. 'Then what are our names?'

'You're Nelvin, and she's Rhubarb. That one over there is Yoshi.'

'My name's not Nelvin, it's Melvin,' said Melvin.

'Yeah, I just said that to annoy you,' said the Donut Graffiti Demon, and I did a little sniggle, even though it wasn't really the time for sniggling.

'And who are you?' I asked.

The man glanced around the room. 'Erm . . . I'm Arch . . . ie,' he said. 'Archie . . . Clamp.'

Rhubarb rolled her eyes and pointed to the smashed-through doorway. It was sort of arched at the top and next to it a clamp held two scaffolding poles together.

'You expect us to believe that?' she said, pointing at the arch and the clamp.

The Donut Graffiti Demon shrugged. 'That's just a coincidence,' he said.

I peered down at his feet. I don't know why, I just did. He was wearing a pair of silver trainers with 'HOVER BOOT' written on each one.

So that's how he'd been hovering. 'What are you, from the future or something?' I asked.

'You guessed it, Yoshi!' said the old man. 'How do you like my new teeth, by the way?' He squeezed his earlobe and they went from glowing white to bright blue.

Melvin stared at the Donut Graffiti Demon's teeth. 'You're from the future?' he said.

Rhubarb tutted. 'He just told us that, you dimwit.'

'Can you please stop calling me a dimwit,' said Melvin.

Rhubarb stroked her chin and stared at the old man. 'What I want to know is why you've been spraying all these words around town.'

She pulled a little black notepad out of her pocket that looked exactly like my old one.

'Hey, you copied my notepad!' I said.

Rhubarb Plonsky

SOME-THING STINKS & THAT'S OK!

BE NOSEY

'Well somebody has to take notes,' said Rhubarb. 'And you're too busy staring at your phone the whole time.'

She flipped to a page and held it up.
Scribbled down were all the words the
Donut Graffiti Demon had sprayed
around Donut, numbered from one to five:

1. WASHING POWDER
2. SLICE OF TOAST
2. MILK CARTON
3. ICE CREAM
5. WATER BOTTLE

Rhubarb pointed at it and
stared at the old man.
'What is this, some kind of
shopping list?' she said.

The Donut Graffiti Demon shook his head all seriously. 'No, it's not a shopping list, Rhubarb,' he said.

'Then what is it?' I asked.

'That's for you to work out,' said the man.

Rhubarb sniffed the air. 'You're giving us a mystery?' she said. 'But why?'

'That's for you to work out,' said the man.

'You already said that,' said Melvin. He turned to Rhubarb. 'He already said that.'

'You already said that, Melv,' I said, and the Donut Graffiti Demon chuckled, then swivelled round to face the glass case again.

He pulled something out of his pocket and held it up to his nose. 'Good luck, gang,' he said. 'But remember, you must return before nightfall.'

'Before nightfall?' said Melvin. 'But why?'

Archie Clamp took a deep breath then fizzled into thin air.

'He . . . he just disappeared!' I cried.

'Smelly eraser!' said Rhubarb. 'He smelt a smelly eraser!'

I looked at her. 'You're telling me he's got magic fizzling smelly erasers too?' I said. 'This is getting Super Weird!'

'Certainly is,' said Rhubarb, looking around the Prehistoric Hall. 'But why did the Donut Graffiti Demon lead us HERE?'

I glanced around at the glass cases. One was filled with dinosaur-footprint fossils. Another with T-Rex teeth. There was a large glass case on the other side of the room with what looked like rugby balls inside it. 'Fossilised dinosaur eggs,' I said, remembering the nest from earlier.

I swivelled my head back round to look inside the case nearest us. And that's when I spotted something familiar.

Brenda returns

'Brenda!' I said. The little spotlight inside the glass case was pointing straight at a lump of amber about the size of a squished tennis ball. Floating inside it was a familiar looking white rectangle.

Melvin stared at the lump of amber too. 'Brenda the Eraser?' he said. 'But how did you get inside that amber?'

I don't know why he was talking to her like that. Everyone knows erasers can't speak.

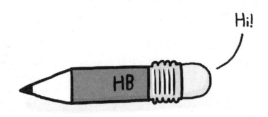

Hi!

I rewound my brain to half an hour before, when we'd been running through the rainforest with a mummy T-Rex chasing after us.

'I dropped it back in the dinosaur times, remember?'

Rhubarb clicked her fingers. 'It must've been fossilised inside some tree sap after we kasplonkled ourselves back,' she said.

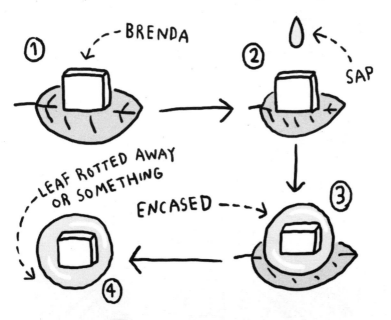

Melvin shook his head. 'Super Weird,' he said. 'It doesn't look a day older.'

'But why did the Donut Graffiti Demon lead us to it?' said Rhubarb.

'I have absolutely no idea,' I said, twizzling round on the spot and heading out of the Prehistoric Hall, towards the next chapter.

No connection

'Where are you going, Yoshi?' said Melvin, following me out of Donut Museum. Rhubarb was right behind him.

'There's more light out here,' I said, whipping my phone out of my pocket and pressing record.

Rhubarb rolled her eyes. 'This is no time for one of your silly little videos,' she said.

'They're not silly,' I said. 'I've had some extremely nice comments about them, thank you very much.'

'Nice comments?' said Melvin. 'I almost had my bum bitten off by a T-Rex thanks to your dad's smelly erasers, and you're talking about nice comments?!'

I ignored Melvin and smiled into the camera. 'Hello Daily Donut fans, this is Yoshi Fujikawa,' I said. 'I just got zapped a week into the future and bumped into the Donut Graffiti Demon. He lured me into Donut Museum where I discovered . . .'

I paused to make it feel more dramatic . . .

'Brenda the Eraser, fossilised inside a lump of amber!'

'Hey, me and Rhubarb were there too, you know,' said Melvin.

I ignored him and pressed the upload button.

'You do realise that none of your viewers will have any idea what you're talking about, don't you?' said Rhubarb.

'That's what keeps them watching, Rubes,' I said in my unfunny old granny voice. 'It's called suspense, my dear girl!'

A big red cross appeared on the screen of my phone.

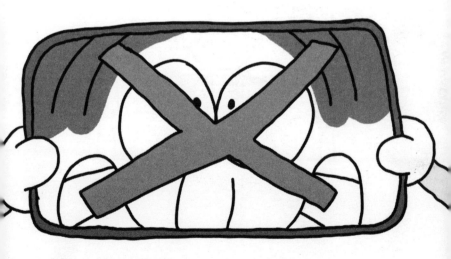

'WHAT?' I cried. 'Still no connection!'

Rhubarb stroked her chin. 'Maybe it's because we've been zapped a week into the future,' she said.

'I don't see why that'd stop his phone working,' said Melvin.

'Yeah, why would that stop . . .' I stopped talking and stared across the street.

Somebody very familiar was walking along the pavement.

'O-over there,' I said, pointing.

My hand was shaking and my legs were wobbling.

Melvin and Rhubarb peered across the street and gasped.

Future Yoshi

'It's you!' cried Melvin.

But how could I be looking at myself?
For a millisecond I thought I'd gone
completely doolally.

And then I realised.

'It's FUTURE me!'
I said.

We all watched as one-week-in-the-future Yoshi Fujikawa strolled down the street wearing a cap with something written on the front of it.

Rhubarb and Melvin were behind me - behind the future version of me, I mean.

They were wearing caps too.

'There's future me!' squealed Rhubarb. 'Hey look, I'm scribbling something in my notepad!'

'And I'm drinking a can of cola,' said Melvin, gawping at himself. 'That's me over there drinking a future can of cola!'

'No wonder your phone doesn't work, Yoshi,' said Rhubarb, clicking her fingers. 'We've been zapped into a completely different dimension!'

Melvin scrunched his face up. 'Different dimension?' he said.

Rhubarb nodded and pointed at our future selves. 'That's us lot if we hadn't been zapped one week into the future,' she explained.

'You mean if we'd just carried on living our lives?' I said.

'Exactly,' said Rhubarb. 'In this dimension, your dad didn't go up into your loft and bring down his smelly erasers.'

Melvin scratched his bum where the T-Rex had been snapping at it. 'I think I prefer this dimension,' he said. 'Hey, let's go say hello!'

He started walking off towards his future self. 'Coowee, Future Me-ee!' he called, waving.

Rhubarb stroked her chin. 'That's probably not a good idea,' she said. 'I've read about people bumping into their future selves. It tends to end badly.'

'How badly?' I asked.

'Usually one of their heads explodes,' said
Rhubarb. 'Sometimes it's both.'

I grabbed her and Melvin and dragged
them behind one of the pillars in front of
Donut Museum. 'We can't let them see us!'
I whispered.

Rhubarb peeked round the pillar. 'What are
those caps we're all wearing?' she said.

I zoomed my eyes in on the cap on top of my head:

Donut Cola Factory

'Hey, we must've just been on a visit to the new factory!' I said.

'Ooh, that sounds like fun,' said Melvin.

My future self pulled his phone out of
his pocket and held it up. 'This is Yoshi
Fujikawa,' he said, talking into its camera.
'And I've just been on a visit to the Donut
Cola Factory!'

'Do I always talk that loud?' I said, surprised
I could hear myself from across the street.
It was just as well I suppose, seeing as it
meant I could hear me.

Future Rhubarb rolled her eyes as she and
Future Melvin followed Future Yoshi down
the road. 'What's this got to do with the
Daily Donut?' she said, very loudly too.
'A visit to the
Donut Cola
Factory isn't
exactly a
mystery,
is it?'

Future Yoshi uploaded his video to Donut
Tube and twizzled round on the spot to
face Future Rhubarb. 'Mystery schmystery,'
he said. 'I got you that cap for free,
didn't I?'

'And this can of Donut Cola,' said Future
Melvin, taking a gulp. 'Thanks Yoshi, it's
delish!'

'No problemo,' said Future Yoshi. 'What did I
tell you? The more followers I get on Donut
Tube, the more free stuff we get!'

Future Rhubarb whipped her cap off as they strolled round a corner. 'Yeah well, I don't want this stupid cap,' she said. 'I want to sniff out a new mystery!'

I waited until they'd gone far enough so they wouldn't hear me. 'Did you hear that?' I said.

'Hear what?' said Melvin.

'What Rhubarb just said,' I said. 'About sniffing out a new mystery. It's given me an idea. Rhubarb, pass me your notepad, would you?'

Rhubarb handed her notepad over and I flicked though, stopping at the page with all the Donut Graffiti Demon's words scribbled on it.

I unzipped my rucksack, pulled out the pencil case and dumped its contents on to the floor. Then I looked at the page in her notepad again:

1. WASHING POWDER
2. SLICE OF TOAST
2. MILK CARTON
3. ICE CREAM
5. WATER BOTTLE

'If I'm not mistaken, there's a few of them in my dad's smelly-eraser collection,' I said.

We all stared at the pile of smelly erasers. Sure enough, amongst them sat:

① a little box of washing powder

② a mini slice of toast

③ a tiny milk carton

④ a teeny ice cream

⑤ a weeny bottle of water

'That's a coincidence,' said Melvin. 'Small world, innit.'

I did my serious face, which is just my normal face, but more serious. 'It's no coincidence,' I said.

Rhubarb scrunched her face up. 'But how did the Donut Graffiti Demon know Yoshi had those smelly erasers in his pencil case?' she asked.

I scooped the smelly erasers back into my pencil case, all except the washing-powder one. I held it in the air.

'I have no idea,' I said, as we all leaned our noses in, getting ready to take a sniff. 'But we're about to find out.'

GIANT "BUBBLE" MONSTER

'Nothing happened,' said Melvin, once we'd been kasplonkled for the nineteenth time that morning.

We were still hiding behind a pillar by the entrance to Donut Museum, exactly where we'd been a second before.

'Hey, what's that banner up there?' said Rhubarb, pointing at a bright red banner hanging above the entrance.

CELEBRATING MONTHS SINCE OUR HALL WAS

Melvin squinted at the banner. 'Who hangs a banner up to celebrate a thing like that?'

'Who cares,' I said. 'It means we've been zapped two months into the future!'

'Roughly,' said Rhubarb.

ROUGHLY 2 PREHISTORIC REDECORATED

Melvin glanced down at Donut High Street. 'The future,' he said. 'Just look at it!'

I looked at the High Street. It seemed pretty much the same to me. An old granny was hobbling along the pavement and a pigeon was pecking at a chip.

Rhubarb sniffed the air. 'Shouldn't we be able to smell washing powder?' she said. 'Like the way the air smelt of cola last time we were kasplonkled?'

I waggled my nostrils. 'Hey, I think I can smell some,' I said.

'Over there!' said Melvin, pointing down the road.

The door of Donut Launderette was open and a giant bubble monster was wobbling out of it.

'Giant bubble monster!' cried a voice, and I spotted Future Rhubarb running down Donut High Street towards the launderette. Future Melvin was following behind her.

'Hey, where's future me?' I said. 'I can only see you two.'

Future Rhubarb whipped her notepad out and started scribbling something down. 'This is Super Weird,' she said in her extra-loud voice.

'It's not THAT weird,' I whispered to Normal Rhubarb and Melvin. 'Somebody probably just put too much washing powder in a machine.'

Future Melvin was taking photos of the bubble monster with a rubbish-looking little camera. 'I wish Yoshi was here,' he said. 'He could be filming this on his phone.'

'Yeah well, he isn't here, is he,' said Future Rhubarb. 'He's back at Brenda the Hut, doing one of his videos, as per usual.'

I twizzled my head round to Normal Rhubarb and Melvin. 'Did you hear that?' I said. 'I'm doing a video in Brenda the Hut. Let's go check it out!'

'But I want to see what happens with the bubble monster,' said Melvin.

I peered over at the monster, which was still spewing through the door of the launderette. An old granny appeared from inside its bubbly body, holding a basket of washing. 'I've lost me knickers,' she warbled.

'This is definitely where the action is,' said Rhubarb, all seriously.

'Yeah well, I've got the magic fizzling smelly erasers, haven't I,' I said, heading off towards Brenda the Hut. 'So unless you wanna be stuck here forever, you'd better follow me!'

Back to Brenda

Three and three-quarter minutes later I skidded to a stop outside Brenda the Hut.

'I can't believe you've dragged us all the way over here when there's a perfectly good Bubble Monster Mystery to investigate on Donut High Street,' said Rhubarb.

'Shhh!' I whispered, peering through the dusty window and spotting Future Me sitting at a little desk. I'd propped my phone up against the pottery crocodile dog thingy on the little shelf and was pressing the record button.

'Yoshi Fujikawa here,' I said - my future
self said, that is. 'And welcome to another
episode of Yoshi's Universe!'

'Hey, you copied Roland's Room!' whispered
Melvin. 'Apart from the "Room" bit.
And the "Roland's" bit.'

Future Yoshi was holding up a little rectangle-shaped packet of cards. 'Today I've been sent these amazing stickers by the very generous people at Donut Supermarket,' he said.

'Ooh, collectable stickers,' I whispered. 'That sounds good.'

My future self ripped the packet open and pulled out five cards. 'Each card features a famous landmark on Donut Island,' he said, holding one up. 'Here's the well known leaning lamppost of Donut High Street.'

Melvin yawned. 'This is boring,' he whispered. 'Can't we go back to the launderette now?'

'Back to the launderette?!' I whispered back. 'Can you even hear yourself?'

Future Yoshi held up another card. 'Ooh look, this is the bench outside the library,' he said. 'Remember, these amazing stickers are only available at Donut Supermarket. You get a free packet with every ten pounds your mum spends!'

Rhubarb copied Melvin's yawn. Or maybe she made it up herself.

'Do you mind?' I said. 'I'm watching myself do a video over here.'

Rhubarb turned to Melvin. 'I'm so glad that old Archie Clamp bloke from the future sent us on this exciting mystery adventure, aren't you, Melv?'

Melvin sniggled. 'Yeah, I wouldn't've missed this for the UNIVERSE!'

'SHHH!' I whisper-shouted, pointing at my future self. 'For all you know, Future Yoshi IS the mystery.'

'Yeah, The amazing Mystery of Why We're Standing Here Wasting Our Time Watching Him Do A Boring Old Video About Stickers,' said Rhubarb. She stuffed her hand into her pocket and whipped her notepad out, then turned to the page with the list on it:

1. ~~WASHING POWDER~~
2. SLICE OF TOAST
2. MILK CARTON
3. ICE CREAM
5. WATER BOTTLE

'What are you up to now?' I said.

'Getting us out of here, dear,' said Rhubarb in her granny voice, which is even worse than mine. 'Melvin, be so kind as to unzip Yoshi's rucksack, would you, love.'

Melvin peered at the list in Rhubarb's notepad and smiled. 'I like your thinking, Rubes!' he said, scuttling round behind me and unzipping my rucksack.

(un)Ziiiiiiiiiip!

'Hey, nobody unzips my rucksack except for me,' I said. 'And future me, I suppose.'

Rhubarb stuck her hand into my rucksack. She pulled out my pencil case, then unzipped that too.

'Smelly eraser number two,' she said, grabbing the mini slice of toast and holding it up to my nose. She and Melvin leaned their hooters in too. 'Take a deep breath and this'll all be over.'

'I will not,' I said, pincering my nostrils shut.

'Fine,' said Rhubarb. 'Then we'll just kasplonkle without you.'

'GAAAH!' I growled, de-pincering my nostrils and breathing in.

One year later

There was a great big kasplonkle then it all went quiet again. We were still standing in the tiny forest, right next to Brenda the Hut.

I peered through the dusty window, but it was empty. 'Looks like everybody's out,' I said.

A photo of the bubble monster from Donut Launderette had been propped up against the jam jar on the shelf.

'Mystery unsolved?' said Rhubarb, staring at the photo. 'But we've never not solved a case before!'

'Hey, what year are we in?' said Melvin, and I peered through the window of Brenda again, trying to read the date on the little digital clock sitting on the desk.

'OMG,' I said. 'We've been zapped forward a year this time!'

Suddenly Rhubarb gasped. 'Smoke!' she cried, pointing in the direction of the Donut Cola Factory. Sure enough, black clouds were billowing up into the sky from behind the trees in the little forest.

'Quick, let's go!' cried Melvin, heading off towards the giant hole.

Giant toast

We skidded to a stop next to an enormous rectangle-shaped slot that'd appeared in the ground near the giant hole.

Black smoke was billowing out of it and a crowd had gathered round. In the distance I could hear a fire engine hurtling towards us.

'What is that thing?' I said, peering down into the slot.

'Some kind of new hole,' said Rhubarb. 'Except rectangle-shaped instead of a circle.'

Just then the most almighty ping echoed though the air, followed by a humungous slice of toast shooting out of the slot.

WHOOSH!

'GIANT TOAST!' screamed an old granny who'd been standing near us, watching.

'Ooh that reminds me, I haven't had any breakfast,' said her friend, who was standing next to her.

The enormous slice loop-the-looped in mid-air, hovered for a millisecond, then crashed on top of the one-year-old Donut Cola Factory.

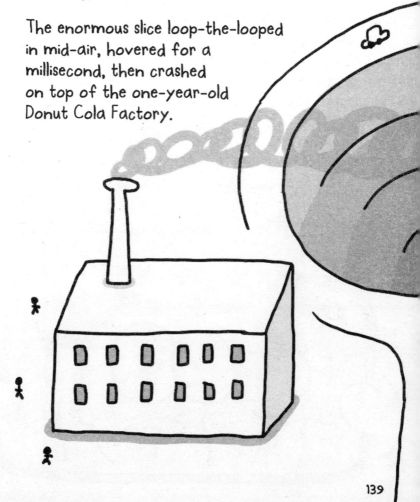

The crowd started running, their arms waggling in the air.

I whipped my phone out of my pocket and pressed record. 'This is Yoshi Fujikawa and I've been zapped a whole year into the future. A giant slice of toast has just popped out of the ground and landed on top of the Donut Cola Factory!'

'I don't know why you're filming yourself,' said Rhubarb, running over to the Donut Cola Factory with Melvin. 'You can't upload it, remember?'

'I'm saving it for when we get back,' I said, following them.

'That's IF we get back,' said Rhubarb, skidding to a stop a few metres from the factory, and I was just about to ask her what she meant when I spotted a familiar face.

TURN PAGE TO SEE FACE →

"Mr Fujikawa goes doolally"

'D-dad?' I said, because my dad was standing right next to me, staring up at the slice of toast that was balancing on the Donut Cola Factory's roof.

He looked older, which wasn't surprising really, seeing as we'd been zapped a year into the future.

'Hello there you three,' he said, looking slightly shocked. 'What a pleasant surprise to see you all together again.'

Rhubarb scrunched her face up. 'Back together again?' she said, but my dad just stood there smiling at us.

'How about that giant slice of toast, eh?' said my dad. 'Should make a good story for your little newspaper.'

Melvin nodded. 'You're not kidding,' he said.

My dad stared at me. 'You look younger, son,' he said. 'Must be all this fresh air you're getting. It really is lovely to see you out and about.'

What was he talking about?

'Ha, ha, yeah, fresh air,' I said, even though the air stank of toast.

Just then I spotted Rhubarb and Melvin
running towards us.

'Huh?' I said, seeing as Rhubarb
and Melvin were standing next
to me.

Then I remembered we'd been zapped into
another dimension and there were two
of us each here.

'Er, got to go, Dad,' I said, grabbing my
pals and darting behind a particularly wide
tree trunk.

Future Rhubarb and Future Melvin peered up at the giant slice of toast. 'What happened here?' cried Future Rhubarb.

My dad twizzled round on the spot and did a little yelp. 'How did you do that?' he said.

'Do what, Mr Fujikawa?' said Future Melvin. 'Long time no see, by the way. How's Yoshi doing?'

My dad blinked. 'Wasn't he just here with you two?'

'We haven't seen him in weeks,' said Future Rhubarb. 'Apart from at school of course, but he keeps himself to himself.'

'I think I must be going doolally,' said my dad, strolling off looking all confused.

He wasn't the only one who was confused.

Future Rhubarb whipped her notepad out and scribbled something down. 'The Mystery of The Giant Slice Of Toast That Crashed Into The Donut Cola Factory,' she said. 'What do you reckon of that for a title, Melv?'

Future Melvin shrugged. 'Not bad,' he said. 'Yoshi would've come up with something snappier though.'

'Yeah well, he isn't here, is he?' snapped Future Rhubarb. 'Now, let's try and work out what happened.'

I stared at my future pals. 'So where AM I then?' I muttered to myself.

Well, I was about to find out, wasn't I.

Roland from Roland's Room

'Hey look, it's Roland from Roland's Room!'
said Melvin, peering round the trunk of the
tree we were hiding behind.

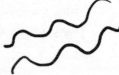

Roland was strolling past, staring at his phone. It was about twice the size of a normal phone, which made it much easier to see the screen from where I was hiding. I zoomed my eyes in on it and gasped. 'OMG, he's watching ME!' I whispered to Normal Rhubarb.

'By Jiminy, he is as well,' she said.

I looked a bit older on the screen - about a year older, to be exact. I was standing in what looked like a little TV studio and there was a Yoshi's Universe logo hanging off the ceiling behind me.

'Looks like you've gone professional,' said Melvin, who was staring at Roland's screen as well.

'Yoshi Fujikawa here,' crackled my voice out of Roland's little speaker. 'Welcome to Yoshi's Universe!'

'Urgh, I hate this kid,' said Roland.

'Today I have something very special to show you,' said my future self. I held up a flashy looking white box with 'Donut Fone' written on it. 'Courtesy of my friends at Donut Electronics!'

The old granny who hadn't had her breakfast sneered over at Roland's phone and tutted. 'These young'uns with their phones,' she said. 'Turn the blooming thing down, would you!'

Her granny friend chuckled. 'Let's get you home for a bite to eat, Mildred,' she said. 'We all know what you're like when you're hungry.'

Roland had stopped walking now and was standing there scratching his bum, staring at the screen, completely unaware of the giant slice of toast stuck in the roof of the factory next to him.

'Ooh, look at this!' crackled my voice out of his speaker as I pulled the lid off the box. 'A brand new Donut Fone!'

I pulled a circular phone with a hole in the middle of it out of the box. To be honest, it was the stupidest looking thing I'd ever seen.

Roland grunted. 'Argh, that's not fair!' he said. 'That Donut Fone shoulda been mine!'

Just then a little girl walked up to Roland and poked him in the bum.

'Hey, aren't you that Roland's Room bloke from Roland's Room?' she asked.

'So what if I am?' snapped Roland, secretly looking a tiny bit pleased to be recognised.

'What happened to you?' asked the little girl. 'You used to be all over Donut Tube.'

Roland held his phone up so the little girl could see the screen. 'Yoshi Fujikawa,' he said. 'That's what happened.'

'Ooh, I love Yoshi's Universe,' said the little girl. 'His unboxing videos are the best!'

I nudged Melvin. 'Did you hear that?' I said. 'I'm famous!'

Suddenly a strange creaking sound echoed through the sky above us.

I looked up and spotted the giant slice of toast starting to crack in half down the middle.

'Everybody stand back!' cried a fireman who'd arrived and was holding a great big hose. I don't know why he was holding a hose, seeing as there wasn't a fire. Although the toast was slightly on the burnt side, I have to admit.

Future Melvin, who'd been standing nearby with Future Rhubarb, staring at the giant slice, twizzled round on the spot and started running off. 'Come on Rubes, let's get out of here before we're toast!' he cried.

Normal Melvin chuckled. 'Did you hear my toast joke?' he whispered to me and Rhubarb, but we just ignored him.

I stared at Future Rhubarb. 'I'm not going anywhere,' she said to Future Melvin. 'This is the biggest mystery to hit Donut Island in weeks!'

The giant slice of toast creaked again and Normal Melvin stopped chuckling at his rubbish joke. 'Hang on a millisecond, how are we gonna get out of here without our future selves spotting us?' he whispered. 'If that slice falls, we really ARE toast!'

Normal Rhubarb stroked her chin as giant crumbs started to fall through the air, crashing to the ground and exploding into smaller, but still quite large, crumbs.

Roland from Roland's Room turned and walked off, and I watched my face disappear into the distance.

Rhubarb whipped her notepad out and flipped it open to the list:

'Yoshi, pass me your pencil case,'
said Rhubarb.

Melvin clicked his fingers. 'Of course!' he said.
'We can zap ourselves out of here with a
smelly eraser!'

Rhubarb nodded. 'Number three on the list
was the milk carton, wasn't it?'

I fished the milk carton out of the pencil
case and held it up in front of our noses.

'Next stop, kasplonkle-ville,'
said Melvin, and we all leaned in.

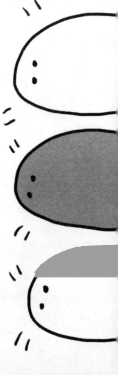

An udder crazy mystery

The first thing I noticed, once we'd been kasplonkled by the milk-carton smelly eraser, was that the sky had got a tiny bit darker. It was a little bit misty too.

'Hey, it's got a tiny bit darker,' I said, saying what I'd just noticed. 'And a little bit misty too.'

'That's not good,' said Rhubarb. 'Remember what that Archie Clamp bloke said?'

'You must return before nightfall,' said Melvin, doing his old man impression, which I had to admit was pretty good.

I scrunched my face up. 'Why DO we have to return before nightfall?' I said.

'Who knows,' said Rhubarb. 'But I don't really want to find out.'

We looked around. The Donut Cola Factory was still there, but it didn't look the same. Its windows were all broken and the roof had completely collapsed. Growing out of its bricks were what seemed to be loads of wobbly cow udders.

I took a step backwards and my trainer landed into something squidgy. Half the floor was covered in udders too.

SQUODGE

'What year is this, two thousand and udder?' I said.

Melvin clicked his fingers. 'The milk-carton smelly eraser!' he said. 'Milk comes from udders!'

Just then, an old granny carrying a shopping bag hobbled past. 'Good, innit!' she said. 'You can't beat a glass of nice warm milk, can you?'

'I have to admit, I do like a glass of milk,' said Melvin, as I stared at the old granny. I was trying to work out if she was the same one as before - the one who hadn't eaten breakfast. But all old grannies look the same to me . . .

Rhubarb sniffed the air. 'This is udder madness,' she said.

The old granny chuckled. She whipped a glass out of her bag and squeezed the teat of an udder growing out of a nearby bollard. White liquid dribbled into the glass.

She guzzled down the bubbly beverage and wiped her mouth. "Ere, 'aven't got any toilet rolls, 'ave ya?' she asked. 'Just been down Donut Supermarket but it's closed.'

Rhubarb shook her head. 'Er, no, sorry,' she said.

'Best be off to Smelly Side Supermarket then,' said the old lady, doing a milk burp. 'It's desperate times, I'm telling ya!'

'Erm, OK, have a nice time,' said Melvin as we headed off towards Donut High Street, which was just across the page in the next chapter.

Teenage Rhubarb

'I can't believe this is Donut High Street,' I said, as we walked down it. The whole blooming road was covered in udders. I whipped my phone out and started filming. 'This is gonna make the best Donut Tube video ever!'

Melvin had strolled over to Donut Pizza and was reading a poster stuck up in the window:

FREE
MILK
SHAKES
DUE TO ALL THE UDDERS.

'This is my lucky day!' he said, disappearing into the restaurant and reappearing three seconds later, sucking on a straw.

'You sure you should be drinking that?' said Rhubarb, but Melvin just ignored her.

I glanced about. 'This is Super Duper Weird,' I said. 'There's nobody around at all!'

'Maybe they're all down Smelly Side Supermarket looking for toilet rolls,' said Rhubarb.

'You know what I've noticed?' said Melvin, sucking on his milkshake. 'Things seem to be getting weirder every time we kasplonkle ourselves into the future.'

'Yeah, I noticed that too,' said Rhubarb, and I tried to think of something I'd noticed.

'Hey, we still don't know what year it is,'
I said, but nobody seemed to notice. They
were too busy listening to a screeching sound
coming from the other end of the street.
Two van headlights were glaring in the
mist, zooming closer and closer to us by
the millisecond.

'Quick, hide!' said Rhubarb, dragging me and
Melvin behind a particularly wide lamppost.

'Look how wide lampposts have got in the future!' I said. Then I realised it was just the udders growing out of it that made it look so thick.

The beaten-up old van, which was covered in wobbly pink udders, screeched to a halt outside Donut Supermarket.

The side door slid open and Future Rhubarb jumped out. 'OMG Rubes,' I gasped. 'You've turned into a teenager!'

Future Teenage Rhubarb was about three cans of Donut Cola taller than her normal self and had sprayed her hair blue. That or it'd turned blue by itself, but I reckon her spraying it was more likely. She was wearing an all-in-one plastic zip-up jump suit.

'Pretty cool!' whispered Normal Rhubarb, staring at herself. Then Future Teenage Melvin jumped out of the van.

He was even taller than Future Rhubarb. His hair was cut short on top but had been left to grow long at the back. His nose had gone all big and greasy and his earlobes were filled with about a million earrings.

'That can't be me,' whispered Normal Melvin, sounding disappointed.

I peered through the window of the driver's seat, excited to see if I was the one driving the van. But instead of me, all I could see was blooming old Roland from Roland's Room.

'No me,' I said. 'Again!'

'Meet us on the Smelly Side,' boomed Future Melvin to Roland in a deep voice, and Roland nodded.

'You got it, Melv,' he said, and the beaten-up old van skidded off into the mist.

Toilet rolls

'Now to find some toilet rolls,' said Future
Rhubarb. She pulled a great big torch off
her belt and shone it through the window of
Donut Supermarket.

Donut Torch Corp'

Normal Rhubarb stared at herself.
'Everyone's obsessed with toilet rolls!'
she whispered.

'It's a mystery,' whispered Normal Melvin.

'The Mystery of Why Nobody Seems To Have Any Toilet Rolls,' I said, and Melvin chuckled.

'You've still got it, Yosh,' he said.

Future Melvin was peering over Future Rhubarb's shoulder. They seemed to be staring at the toilet-roll aisle of Donut Supermarket. 'The shelves are all empty,' he said.

Toi

Just then, an almighty ping echoed though the air. 'TOAST!' boomed Future Melvin, and he and Rhubarb covered their heads. I stared into the sky and spotted a giant slice of slightly burnt toast hurtling over our heads.

'THAT's still happening?' I whispered to Normal Rhubarb. 'But this is years later!'

Normal Rhubarb shrugged. 'Looks like we never solved the toast mystery either,' she said.

'And now our future selves are traipsing around looking for toilet rolls,' whispered Normal Melvin. 'What's happened to good old Donut Island?'

Future Rhubarb and Future Melvin headed off down Donut High Street, towards the giant hole, and we stepped out from behind the uddery lamppost.

Across the road, in the window of Donut Electronics, a TV screen was flickering. The person on it looked kind of familiar.

He had bouncy black hair and glasses and a face exactly like mine except more teenagerish.

'Yoshi, that's you!' said Rhubarb, and we all ran across the street, taking care not to step on any udders.

Yoshi's Universe

'Hey there, Yoshi Fujikawa fans, and welcome to Yoshi's Universe!' said the me on TV as we skidded to a stop outside Donut Electronics. Luckily the TV volume was really high.

'OMG I've got my own TV show now!'
I said, staring at myself.

'Today I'll be unboxing something very
special,' said Future Teenage Me.
'I'm sure you'll all be very jealous!'

TV me held up a cardboard box and lifted
the lid off. Then he pulled out a toilet roll.

'Yes, that's right, it's a toilet roll,' he said.
'Told you you'd be jealous!'

Melvin stared at the TV. 'Again with
toilet rolls?' he said.

Definitely seems to be a shortage of them. Maybe that's why Archie Clamp sent us to the future

said Rhubarb.

'What, to hunt down a secret stash of loo paper?' I said. 'No, I'm sure it must have something to do with me.'

I pointed at the TV screen. My future self was unfurling the roll of toilet paper and rubbing it against his cheek. His face cheek, not his bum one.

'Mmm, lovely soft toilet paper,' he said. 'Don't you wish you had some too?'

Rhubarb looked at me - the normal me, not the me on the telly. 'What have you become, Yoshi?' she said.

'Don't blame me,' I said. 'I'm not him!'

My future self was still rubbing the toilet roll on his cheek.

If only you were rich like me. Then you could afford some of this delicious three-ply loo roll!

he said.

AVAILABLE AT DONUTSUPERMARKET.com
HURRY WHILE STOCKS LAST!

The TV screen flickered, then turned black.

'Well at least I seem to be doing all right,'
I said.

Yeah, but what
about everyone else?
How are they wiping
their bums?
Have you thought
about that, Yoshi?

I haven't,
to be
honest

Just then, another old granny waddled
past. I swear, it was like old grannies were
the only people who left their houses in the
future.

'Hey, aren't you that Daily Donut lot?' she
said, and we all twizzled round. 'Shouldn't
you be teenagers by now?'

Rhubarb nodded. 'Er yeah, that's us,' she said. 'We're erm, late developers.'

Thought so. I used to like your little newspaper.

'Thanks, missus,' said Melvin. 'But what do you mean you USED to like it?'

The old granny looked at him like he was an idiot. 'They cancelled it years ago,' she said. 'After you stopped solving the mysteries.' She looked around at the udders growing out of everything. 'That's when the REALLY weird stuff started happening.'

A familiar-sounding ping echoed though the air. 'TOAST!' screamed the granny, scuttling off. 'Ooh that reminds me, I haven't had me lunch.'

Ice cream

An enormous, slightly burnt rectangle of sliced bread flew across the sky and crashed into a tree.

Rhubarb stroked her chin. 'After we stopped solving mysteries?' she muttered to herself. 'What was that old lady talking about?'

'Maybe that's the mystery Archie Clamp wants us to solve,' said Melvin. 'The Mystery of Why We Stopped Solving Mysteries . . .'

'Catchy,' I said, and Rhubarb chuckled.

'It's not funny,' said Melvin.

Rhubarb nodded. 'No, it's not,' she said.
'Yoshi, pass me your pencil case, would you?'

She whipped her notepad out and flipped it
open to the list:

I passed her the pencil case.

'I'm beginning to wonder why we keep sniffing these things,' said Melvin. 'It gets worse every blooming time.'

Rhubarb fished around in the pencil case and pulled out the eraser shaped like an ice cream. 'What else can we do?' she said. 'It's the only way we'll find out what happens.'

She held the ice cream up and we all leaned in.

And you can guess what happened next.

'That kasplonkle felt different from the other ones,' I said.

'Yeah, it was more of a kaplonkstle,' said Rhubarb.

I looked around. The high street was still covered in udders but they weren't wobbly any more. They'd turned grey and all dried up. Oh yeah, and it was almost evening now too, which wasn't exactly great, seeing as we weren't supposed to stay out past nightfall, if you remember what Archie Clamp had said.

You must return before nightfall

'Is anyone else feeling a bit nippy?' said Melvin. 'Mainly around the head and neck region?'

I looked at him. Instead of a head, he had a giant upside-down ice cream splodged on top of his body.

'Boy, are you gonna wish you didn't sniff that ice-cream smelly eraser,' I said, sticking my camera in his face.

Melvin twizzled round and stared at his reflection in a shop window. 'WAAAHHH!!!' he screamed. 'I'm a 99!'

'Technically speaking, there has to be a chocolate flake to make it a 99,' I said.

Just then, an old granny doddered past. Yes, I know, another old granny. This one had a great big upside down ice cream for a head as well.

'Evening!' she said, like nothing weird was going on at all.

'Hey, she's got an ice cream for a head too,' I said.

A man was strolling along the pavement on the other side of the road. He had an ice-cream head three.

Rhubarb stroked her chin. 'Maybe it's because you drank that milkshake,' she said. 'I told you not to, Melv.'

'Thanks for that, Rhubarb,' said Melvin.

Suddenly a car drove past. I say drove, it was hovering actually.

'Hey look, a real-life hovering car!' said Melvin. 'We must really be in the future now.'

I had to admit, he seemed to be dealing with having an ice cream for a head pretty well, all things considered.

The car screeched to a stop outside Donut Supermarket and four tyres miraculously fizzled to life in the space underneath it, where the tyres would usually be. Written on each one in great big capital letters was the word 'INVISITYRES'.

'Oh well that's a bit of a letdown,' I said. 'Still pretty cool though.'

'It is pretty cool, isn't it,' said Melvin. I think he'd completely forgotten about his head being an ice cream to be honest.

Rhubarb was staring down at her notepad. 'Can we try and concentrate on The Mystery of Why Archie Clamp Sent Us To The Future?' she said.

Good point, Rhubarb. I still think it's got something to do with me.

'Hey,' said Melvin, pretty much ignoring what I'd just said. 'We haven't seen our future selves yet.'

Right at that exact moment, a man and a woman appeared, pushing a pram. They both had ice-cream heads, and their kid did too.

'Lovely-looking family,' I said, sounding like an old granny. 'Apart from the ice-cream heads, of course.'

'OMG,' said Melvin, staring at the family as they walked off.

Rhubarb looked up from her notepad. 'What is it, Melv?' she asked.

Melvin turned to face Rhubarb and the cone sticking out of his ice-cream head wobbled. 'That was me and you,' he said.

Three seconds later...

'Wait a minute,' said Rhubarb, even though it was only three seconds later. 'Are you telling me those two people were . . . YOU and ME?!'

'YES!' said Melvin. 'Except with ice-cream heads, of course.'

'So we're . . .' said Rhubarb. 'And we've got a . . .'

'YES!' said Melvin.

I chuckled to myself as I filmed Rhubarb's reaction. 'Congratulations!' I said. 'You have a lovely-looking family. Apart from the ice-cream heads.'

Rhubarb looked like she was about to faint. 'Would you put down that blooming phone,' she said.

'You'll thank me when this goes viral on Donut Tube,' I said, and Rhubarb pulled herself together. Not that she'd fallen apart or anything. It's just a saying.

'So at least we know what's happened to me and Melv,' she said. 'But what about you, Yosh?'

I shrugged. 'I just hope I haven't got an ice cream for a head,' I said.

'Why?' said Rhubarb.

'Because I like having a normal head,' I said. I was surprised I had to explain it to her, to be honest.

Rhubarb shook her head. She was pointing down the end of Donut High Street, towards the giant hole.

No, "Y"!

she said.

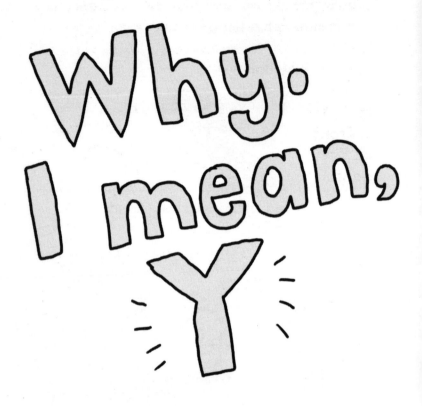

Why.
I mean,
Y

There, hovering above the giant hole, was the most ginormous letter Y I'd ever seen. It seemed to glow from inside and changed colour every few seconds.

'Y!' said Melvin, pointing at me.
'Yoshi, your name starts with a Y!'

We all started running towards it. 'OK Yosh, I'm beginning to think this whole mystery might actually have something to do with you,' said Rhubarb as we skidded to a stop in front of the giant Y.

'Thank you!' I said, pointing my camera at the giant Y. 'I'm glad you're starting to see it from my point of view.'

Now we were closer, I could see that it was some kind of Y-shaped office block. There were different floors inside the mahoosive letter, filled with people sitting at desks, and one big room at the top.

Inside the big room stood a single, solitary
figure. The sun was sinking into the horizon
behind him, turning him into a silhouette.

I say him, it could've been a her. Except
for the fact that there was something
very familiar about this figure.

'I - I think that might be me,' I said,
pointing up at it.

ridgy

Rhubarb looked around. The whole of
Donut Island was pretty much empty apart
from inside the giant Y. 'Yoshi's Universe . . .'
she said. 'You've turned Donut Island into
Yoshi's Universe!'

'Well Yoshi's Island, anyway,' I said.

Melvin stamped his foot. 'So let me get this straight,' he said. 'I'm married to Rhubarb and you're some kind of billionaire?! Well if you ask me, this future STINKS!'

And something about the way he'd said the word 'stinks' made me remember my smelly erasers.

I pulled my pencil case out as I watched the sun, still sinking into the horizon.

'If that sun sinks, we're in big trouble,' I said.

'Why?' said Melvin, and I don't think he was talking about the giant building.

Rhubarb opened her mouth. 'You must return before nightfall,' she said in her rubbish old granny voice, even though Archie Clamp had been a grandad, not a granny.

She whipped her notepad out and it flipped itself open to the list:

'You know what to do, Yosh,' she said, and
I nodded. I stuck my hand into my pencil
case and pulled out the smelly
eraser shaped like a weeny
bottle of water.

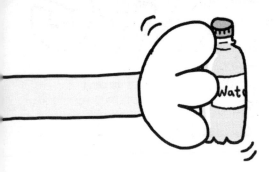

'This is the smelly eraser
I fear the most,' I said, mostly
just to make the moment feel a
bit more dramatic. I mean, what
could be so bad about water?

'What does water even smell like?'
said Melvin.

Rhubarb leaned her hooter in. 'Absolutely
blooming nothing,' she said, taking a great
big sniff anyway.

'The future

'You're right,' I said, once we'd been kasplonkled. 'That smelly eraser didn't smell of anything.'

'Maybe it isn't even a smelly eraser at all,' said Melvin. 'Maybe it's just a plain old eraser and we didn't get zapped anywhere.'

Rhubarb shook her head. 'How do you explain that, then?' she said, nodding at the giant Y building, and I gasped. I'm telling you, I did a LOT of gasps that day.

Next to the Y building there were four new buildings. Together they spelt the word "NOT" with a question mark at the end.

'Y NOT?' said Melvin, reading the buildings out loud. 'Why would you build a load of buildings that said that?'

'Why not?' I said.

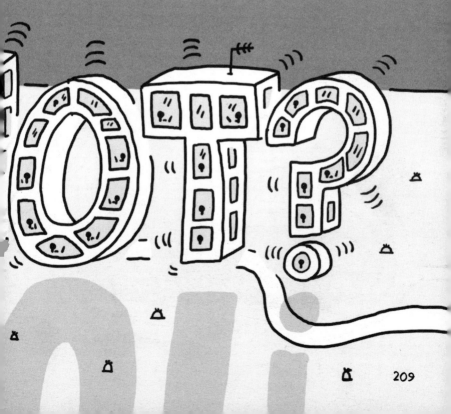

Just then, a raindrop landed on my nose.
I looked up and spotted a great big black
cloud. Suddenly there was the most almighty
explosion in the sky and a bolt of light shot
across it. 'The weeny bottle of water,'
I said. 'It's zapped us into a blooming great
big storm!'

An old granny with an ice-cream head
scuttled past as a giant slice of toast
crashed into a dried-up-udder-covered
lamppost.

Oh yeah, and I bet that bubble monster was still wobbling its way out the door of Donut Launderette. AND I reckon there was still no toilet roll.

'So this is the future, is it?' said Rhubarb, looking around. 'Well done Yoshi, you've made a right old mess of it.'

'What do you mean?' I said. 'This isn't my fault!'

'I'm afraid it is, Yoshi,' said Melvin in his Archie Clamp voice. Except the voice wasn't coming out of Melvin's mouth.

I glanced over at the Y building and spotted the Donut Graffiti Demon walking towards us.

Yoshi's fault

Rain was falling from the sky like bullets. Actually it was more like rain, but there was loads of it and it was coming down really fast. Thunder crackled in the sky above our heads.

'Welcome to the future,' said Archie Clamp, or the Donut Graffiti Demon, or whatever his blooming name was. 'Long time no see!'

He looked even older than the last time we saw him and was carrying a hover walking stick. He was still wearing his hover boots as well, so I don't see why he needed a walking stick - couldn't he just hover around?

'Feels like we saw you just this morning,' said Melvin, and the old man chuckled.

'In some ways you did,' he said, as I held my phone up and pointed it at him.

This isn't funny, "Archie Clamp". Look what's happened to Donut Island!

'I know,' said the Donut Graffiti Demon. 'Terrible, isn't it.'

He looked at me as raindrops shot through the air between us like bullets. Hang on, have I said that already?

'Why are you looking at me?' I said, glancing up at the storm. 'This isn't my fault!'

'I'm afraid it is, Yoshi,' said the Donut Graffiti Demon.

'You already said that in the last chapter,' I said. 'Why do you keep on saying that?'

The old man stared into my eyes, not blinking. A bolt of lightning shot out of a humungous black cloud and struck a passing granny. I mean, a lamppost.

And then I blinked.

'Hey, wait a millisecond,' I said. 'What were you doing inside that giant Y building?'

The Donut Graffiti Demon shrugged. 'I own it,' he said.

'YOU own it?' said Melvin. 'We figured it was Yoshi's.'

The Donut Graffiti Demon smiled as an almighty gust of wind lifted an old granny off the ground and loop-the-looped her in the air, dumping her into the giant hole. Or maybe it was just a leaf.

'Why do you keep smiling and shrugging and staring at me and stuff?' I said, turning to Rhubarb. 'Why does he keep doing that, Rubes? It's giving me the creeps!'

The rain was shooting down like bullets, except made out of water and more raindrop-shaped than bullet-shaped. All of sudden, for no good reason I could see, Rhubarb peered down at Archie Clamp's fingernails.

OMG

she said.

'What?' I said. But it was no good, I'd have to wait until the next chapter to find out.

The next chapter

'OMG,' said Rhubarb, almost like we'd
gone back a few seconds and she was
repeating what she'd just said. 'Yoshi, look
at the Donut Graffiti Demon's fingernails!'

I zoomed my eyeballs in on Archie Clamp's
fingernails and gasped, but
only so that Rhubarb
wouldn't think I was being
thick. The truth was,
I couldn't see anything
except for ten dried-up
old man's fingernails.

'You still don't get it, do you?' said Rhubarb, as an old lady hobbled past.

Blooming wind. Gets on yer blinking nerves, dunnit!

I zoomed my eyeballs in on her fingernails. And that's when everything clicked.

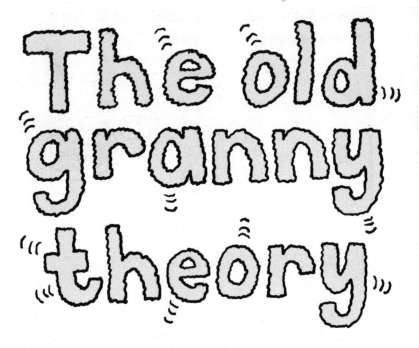

The old granny theory

'OMG,' I said, copying Rhubarb's OMG from twenty seconds before. I pointed at the old granny. 'The old granny!'

'The old granny?' said Melvin. 'What about her?'

'Don't you see?' I said, scrolling through my phone and clicking on a video of an old granny from earlier in the day - the grumpy one who hadn't had her breakfast.

I pressed play and we all watched it
for a minute.

BORINGEST VIDEO EVER...

'Huh?' said Melvin, once it'd finished.

'The old granny!' I said. 'She's been
Archie Clamp all the way through!'

Melvin scrunched
his face up like he
was confused.
I couldn't blame
him, really.
It was a pretty
complicated
theory that only
a very clever
person like me
would understand.

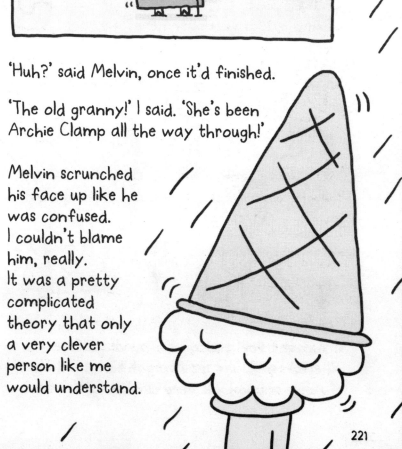

'Archie Clamp here has been dressing up as an old granny and following us through this whole adventure,' I said, explaining my old granny theory. 'No wonder they all looked alike. They were all the same blooming granny!'

Melvin stared at the old granny who'd just hobbled past. 'So how can she be over there if Archie Clamp is over here?' he said.

I thought for a second. 'You've got me there,' I said. 'But you've got to admit, their fingernails do look very similar.'

Rhubarb rolled her eyes. She pointed at Archie Clamp's fingernails. Then she pointed at mine.

'I was talking about YOUR fingernails, you great big dimwit,' she said. 'Archie Clamp's look exactly the same!'

I looked at the Donut Graffiti Demon's fingernails and he gave them a waggle.

I suppose they were kind of ridgy, like mine.

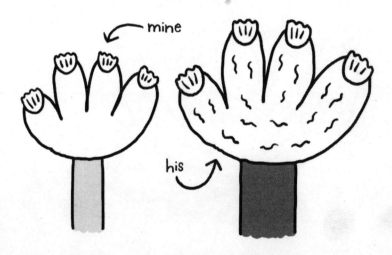

mine

his

'So what?' I said. 'We've got similar-looking fingernails.'

The Donut Graffiti Demon sighed.
'Have I always been this stupid?'
he said to Rhubarb.

And then it really did all click.

'Wait a millisecond,' I said, holding up
my hand and giving it a waggle too.
'So you're . . .'

Me.
I mean . . .
YOU.

'NOOOO!!!!' I wailed, dropping to my knees,
but mainly just to make it all seem a bit
more dramatic.

"STILL
"raining
like
bullets"

The rain really was coming down like bullets now. Only joking, they were still just ordinary raindrops. Quite big ones though. And it was still really windy too. And it was thundering and lightning-ing as well.

'Wait a millisecond, so what's going on?' said Melvin. 'I mean, I completely get it. I could just do with a little round-up, that's all.'

Rhubarb pointed at Archie Clamp.
'He's not called Archie Clamp,' she said.
'Or the Donut Graffiti Demon either.
His name is Yoshi Fujikawa.'

'I can't believe it,' I said.

'Me neither,' said Future Yoshi, bonking me on the head with his hover walking stick.
'I thought you would've worked it out pages ago.'

'Hang on,' said Melvin. 'So Future Yoshi was the one who sent us on this whole great big stupid mystery goose chase in the first place? But why?'

I shrugged.

Future me did, that is.

'To teach myself a lesson,' he said.

'What lesson?' I asked.

Rhubarb was flicking through her notepad. She stopped on a page and started reading out loud.

'They cancelled it years ago,' she said in her old granny voice. 'After you stopped solving the mysteries. That's when the REALLY weird stuff started happening.'

'Isn't that what that old granny said a few kasplonkles ago?' I said. 'About them cancelling The Daily Donut?'

Blah, blah, blah, blah...

Rhubarb nodded. 'As soon as we stopped solving mysteries, the whole of Donut Island started to go Super Duper Weird,' she said.

I scrunched my face up. 'But what's that got to do with me?'

'All the way through this thing, you've been on your blooming phone,' said Rhubarb.

I looked at my phone. 'Yeah, 'cos I've been filming our adventure for Donut Tube,' I said.

'I'm not talking about the normal you,' said Rhubarb. 'I'm talking about the future one.'

I rewound my brain to all the times we'd seen me in the future. It was true, I had been on my phone quite a bit. 'But so what?' I said.

'That's why Future Melvin and me didn't solve any mysteries,' said Rhubarb. 'We didn't have you on the team.'

'Oh please,' I said. 'You and Melvin don't need Yoshi Fujikawa to solve a few mysteries.' I pointed at the giant Y building. 'And besides, look what that phone's turned me into. I'm a blooming billionaire!'

'Squillionaire, actually,' said Future Yoshi. 'But that's not the point.'

'So what is the point?' I said.

'The point,' said Future Me, 'is that a squillion pounds doesn't necessarily make a person very happy.'

I stared at him. I mean me. 'You seem cheerful enough,' I said. 'I've heard you do a few chuckles.'

Future Yoshi shrugged. 'I'm very lonely, Yoshi,' he said, and I looked at him, standing there all rich and on his own.

'Hey wait a minute, where are you two?'
I said, turning to Rhubarb and Melvin.
'Your future selves have usually popped
up by now.'

Future Yoshi looked down at his hover
boots. 'About that,' he said. 'There's
something I think you ought to see...'

Yoshi Island Cemetery

'Ought?' I said, following Future Yoshi.
'Since when did I start saying "ought"?'

We were walking towards Donut Island
Cemetery. I knew what it looked like
because my granny's buried there.
My dad makes us visit her every year
on her birthday. It's completely boring.

'Hey, I know this place, it's Donut Island
Cemetery,' I said, showing off that I knew
it. And then I spotted something. The word
'Donut' in the Donut Island Cemetery sign
had been replaced with the word 'Yoshi'.

Cool! I said.

The future me just shrugged. 'Still didn't make me happy, though,' he said.

'All right, all right, we get the point,' I said. 'You're an extremely lonely and unhappy squillionaire.'

We strolled through the gates and I glanced around. Instead of gravestones, there were these flashy new round plastic see-through tanks with people floating inside.

'It didn't use to look like this,' I said, still showing off that I knew the place.

'So this is how people get buried in the future, is it?' asked Melvin.

Future Yoshi chuckled.
'Not exactly,' he said.
'Nobody dies in the future.'

Rhubarb stroked her chin. 'Nobody dies?' she said. 'So why's there a blooming cemetery?'

'Yeah, and what's with all these tanks?' said Melvin, tapping one. And old granny was floating inside it. Next to her sat an old granddad, snoring in a floating armchair.

'Cooee!' said the granny, giving us a wave.

'People get turned into ghosts,' said Future Yoshi, waving back.

Melvin stared at the old granny. 'Ghosts?' he said.

'Yeah, you know - like Rhubarb's dad,' said Future Yoshi. 'Except they live in these tanks.'

Yoshi's dad, remember?

'Super Weird,' I said, looking at my wrinkled-up, ancient, future self. 'Speaking of ghosts, shouldn't you be one by now?'

'Probably,' said Future Yoshi, staring at the old granny in her tank. 'It'll be lonely, floating in one of these things all by myself, won't it.'

'No different to standing in the window of a giant Y-shaped building,' said Melvin as we carried on strolling through the cemetery. 'What are we doing here, anyway?'

'Follow me,' said Future Yoshi.

He led us down a row of tanks, then hung a left, then a right, then stopped. 'Ta da!' he said.

Inside a tank floated two wrinkled-up old codgers with ice creams for heads.

'Oh for crying out loud,' said Rhubarb. 'That's me and Melvin, isn't it.'

'Hey, that's us two when we were kids!' said Future Ghost Melvin, staring out of the tank. 'What are you two doing here?'

Melvin smiled at his future ghost self. 'Oh you know,' he said. 'Just investigating a mystery.'

Future Ghost Rhubarb peered at me. 'Yoshi?' she said. 'Is that my little Yoshi Fujikawa?'

'Look how sweet you were,' she said. She looked at Future Yoshi. 'And then you got that phone.'

I rolled my eyes. 'Not the blooming phone thing again,' I said.

Future Yoshi looked down at his hover boots for like the nine millionth time that day. 'I could've been in that tank with them,' he said. 'If it wasn't for my phone.'

I stared at Melvin and Rhubarb's future ghost selves, floating in the tank. I had to admit, they did look like they were having quite a nice time.

'OK, OK, I get the point,' I said, clicking my phone off. 'I'll cut down on my screen time. Happy now?'

CLICK

See you later!

Future Yoshi shrugged. 'It's a start, I s'pose.'

Rhubarb chuckled. 'I can't believe this whole mystery has been about an old man wanting to get inside a tank with a couple of ice-cream-headed old codgers.'

'So now's the bit when we zap ourselves back to Brenda the Hut, right?' said Melvin.

back in the good old days

'Right!' I said, stuffing my phone into my pocket.

Rhubarb turned to Future Yoshi. 'There's one thing I still don't get,' she said. 'Why not just tell us all of this was going to happen when we were back in the Prehistoric Hall?'

'Yeah, and how did you know about the smelly erasers?' said Melvin. 'I thought Yoshi's dad didn't bring them down from his loft in this dimension . . .'

Future Yoshi smiled. 'That wouldn't have made for a very interesting book, would it?' he said.

Melvin blinked. 'Book?' he said. 'Who said anything about a book?'

The sun had completely set now and I did a little yelp.

'Yelp,' I said, backing up my yelp, because this was a seriously yelp-worthy moment. 'Didn't you say we had to return before nightfall?'

'Hmm,' said Future Me. 'I forgot about that. Oh well, looks like you're stuck here in the future with me. Bad luck.'

And that's the end of this story.

Not really

'Only joking!' said Future Yoshi.
'No, I just made up that nightfall stuff.
There's no rush.'

Rhubarb rolled her eyes. 'You have got to be kidding me,' she said. 'What are we waiting for then? Let's get kasplonkling!'

'But how?' I said. 'How in the name of Brenda the Hut do we zap ourselves back to Brenda the Hut?'

Melvin scrunched his face up. 'That's a point,' he said. 'There's no smelly eraser to get us home!'

'Ah, but isn't there?' said Future Yoshi.

'No,' said Melvin. 'That's what I just said.'

I unzipped my pencil case and poured out all the smelly erasers. There were plenty in there, but which one would zap up back to where we'd come from?

'We need to work out which one smells
like the day we first met Future Yoshi,'
said Rhubarb.

I rewound my brain, trying to think what
smells had drifted up my nostrils that day.

'First I was sitting at home watching TV,'
I said, looking down at the smelly erasers.
There were none in the shape of my living
room. Or my TV either.

be cool
if there
was,
though

'Then you met us at Brenda the Hut,'
said Rhubarb.

We all stared at the smelly eraser collection.
'Brenda the Hut,' I said, trying to think which
one might smell of her.

wish
I had one
of these

Melvin clicked his fingers. 'Brenda the Eraser!'
he said. 'Surely she'd smell of Brenda the
Hut a little bit? She'd been sitting inside it
long enough.'

remember?

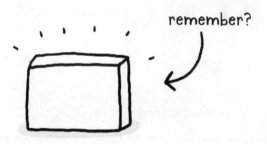

'There's only one problem,' said Rhubarb.
'She isn't in the pile.'

'Oh yeah!' I said. 'She's stuck inside that blooming amber. We have to get to Donut Museum!'

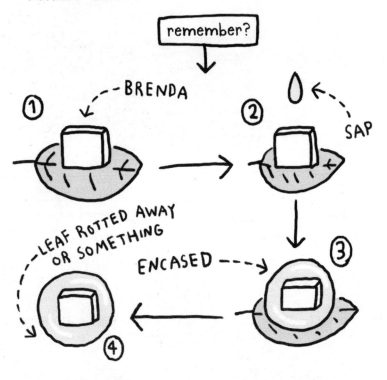

'There's only one problem,' said Future Yoshi. 'It isn't called Donut Museum any more.'

I rolled my eyes. 'Fine, so it's called Yoshi Museum. Sorry, I forgot I owned the island for a second there.'

Future Yoshi bonked me on the head with his hover walking stick. Again.

'Could you stop doing that, please?' I said.

'I'm sorry,' he said.

'Thank you,' I said.

'Not for the bonk,' said Future Yoshi. 'I'm sorry to tell you that Donut Museum was destroyed.'

Rhubarb gasped. 'Destroyed?' she said. 'But how?'

'A giant slice of toast landed on top of it,' said Future Yoshi.

Melvin rolled his eyes. 'That figures,' he said. 'So what are we going to do now?'

'I guess you just give up and live here in the future with me,' said Future Yoshi.

And that really is the end of this story now.

The "hover" walking "stick"

'Or,' said Future Yoshi, 'you could use my hover walking stick!'

Rhubarb looked at him like he was an idiot.

'What, to hover-hobble back in time with?' she said. 'I don't think it works like that, Future Yoshi. You have to have a smelly eraser.'

Future Yoshi held his hover walking
stick up and did one of his sad,
lonely chuckles.

'What if my hover walking stick
was part smelly eraser?' he said,
and we all zoomed our eyes in
on it.

There, at the top of
the walking stick,
stuck on with glue or
something, was the
block of amber with
Brenda the Eraser
inside it.

'Brenda the Eraser!'
cried Melvin. 'Ooh,
you are naughty
teasing us like that,
Future Yoshi!'

'How are we going
to get her out of
that amber though?'
said Rhubarb.

Future Yoshi smiled at me. 'I could bonk him on the head again?'

'No thanks,' I said, grabbing the stick and bonking it against a passing lamppost instead.

'Hang on a millisecond, what's that lamppost doing floating past us?' said Melvin.

'This is the future, you know, Nelvin,' said Future Yoshi, as the amber smashed into a million tiny pieces, and Brenda the Eraser fell on to the floor.

This is the part where, if I could be
bothered, I'd say that Brenda the Eraser
bounced on the pavement then boinged
towards a drain, doinking left and right
over the slots as I dived and grabbed her,
just before she disappeared down into
the sewers.

But I can't be bothered.
So I just bent down and picked her up.

'Right, it's been nice knowing you,' I said to Future Yoshi.

'See you in the future,' he said.

'You mean the mirror,' said Melvin, and we all had a good chuckle. But not for too long.

I held Brenda the Eraser up and leaned my nose towards her. 'Ready, gang?' I said, waggling my nostrils and preparing for one last sniff.

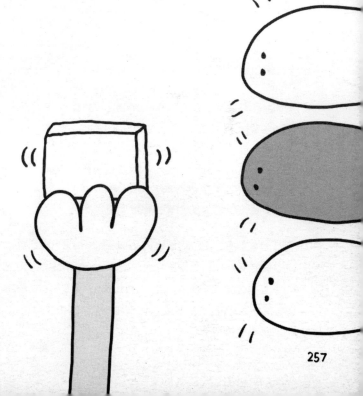

257

"BACK TO" Back to Brenda

'Kasplonkle!' I said, opening my eyes.

'Gesundheit,' said Rhubarb, and I looked around. We were back in good old Donut Island Cemetery.

'Mmm, lovely lovely graves,' I said, as Melvin sniffed the air.

'What I don't get is, how did Brenda the Eraser know to zap us back to the exact right date?' he said. 'I mean, it's not like the whole town smells of Brenda the Hut, is it?'

I shrugged. 'Don't overthink it, Nelvin,' I said.

We walked back to Brenda the Hut and all sat down, even though there was only one chair. 'I'm pooped,' said Rhubarb.

'Me too,' I said. 'Still, there's work to do.' I whipped my pencil case out and dumped the smelly erasers on to the desk.

Melvin stared at them. 'Please don't tell me you're thinking of smelling any of those,' he said.

I chuckled. 'Not right now,' I said, picking up the little dinosaur one and placing it on the shelf, between the jam jar and the pottery crocodile dog thing.

Rhubarb pulled her notepad out. 'S'pose I should start writing up the story,' she said, flipping through it. 'Blimey, I've filled up every page!'

'About that,' I said. 'I was wondering, would you mind if we didn't tell anybody about this one?'

Melvin gasped. 'But it's our greatest mystery ever,' he said. 'Plus you filmed it all on your phone!'

'I know,' I said. 'I just think it'd be better if we let the future happen on its own.'

'Very sensible,' said Rhubarb. 'Now, what are we gonna do with all these erasers?'

'I've got an idea,' I said, I picking up the mini washing-powder box and looking at Rhubarb's notepad.

One last kas-plonkle

I don't know if you've ever rubbed out a whole notepad's worth of scribbles, but I can tell you, it takes a pretty long time. And it uses up a LOT of smelly erasers. Every one of them apart from Brenda the Eraser and the little dinosaur, in fact.

'There,' said Rhubarb, erasing the final word. 'It's completely blank again.'

'Nothing like a nice empty notepad,' I said.

Melvin chuckled. 'I thought you preferred your phone,' he said.

'Ooh, that's a point,' I said. 'I almost forgot.'

I plopped Brenda the Eraser into my pocket then reached over and grabbed the dinosaur smelly eraser off the shelf and gave it a sniff.

I disappeared.

I was back again.

'What was that all about?' asked Rhubarb.

I pulled a bit of rainforest leaf out of my hair. 'Follow me, there's something I want to show you.'

We walked across Donut Island and down Donut High Street, towards Donut Museum.

'Oh bums,' said Melvin, looking in the window of Donut Pizza. 'They're charging for milkshakes again.'

DONUT MUSEUM

UT HAIR

Up the steps of Donut Museum we walked, into the Prehistoric Hall. It was dark and gloomy inside and all round the edge stood glass cases. A single small spotlight shone inside each one.

Scaffolding covered the walls and a doorway had been smashed through one of them into the room next door.

'Sorry for any inconvenience while we make some improvements to the Prehistoric Hall,' said a sign sticky-taped to one of the scaffolding poles.

There was a collection of amber stones inside the glass case nearest us. You know, the sort you see in films when there's a mosquito frozen inside one of them with a smidgen of dinosaur DNA in its dried-up blood.

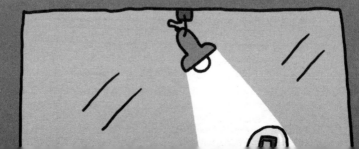

The little spotlight inside the case was pointing straight at a lump of amber a bit bigger than a squished tennis ball. Floating inside it was a familiar looking black rectangle.

'Your phone!' said Rhubarb. 'You kasplonkled yourself back to dinosaur times and dropped your phone on the blooming ground! But why?'

'It was the least I could do,' I said. 'Seeing as you'd rubbed out your notepad and everything.'

'But what about your little films?' asked Melvin. 'I thought you loved making them?'

I stroked my chin. 'If I'm not mistaken, my dad's got an old video camera up in our loft somewhere.'

getting zapped right now

'As long as it doesn't fizzle,' said Melvin.

Rhubarb chuckled. She stuffed her hand into her pocket and pulled out her notepad. 'Thought you might like it,' she said.

'Me?' I said, as she handed it over.

'Yeah, it didn't really suit me anyway,' said Rhubarb.

I opened it up and stared at the first page.

'And now for a brand new mystery,' I said, smiling at my two best friends.

And that's when I realised Melvin still had an ice cream for a head.